First U.S. edition

LIBRARY OF CONGRESS CATALOGING-IN-PUBLICATION DATA

Lieshout, Elle van.
The nothing king / Elle van Lieshout & Erik van Os ; illustrated by Paula Gerritsen.
p. cm.
Summary: King Bear leaves his palace to live with his pet rabbit and
care for his pansy in a simple apartment on the outskirts of town.
ISBN 1-932425-14-4 (alk. paper)
[1. Bears—Fiction. 2. Kings, queens, rulers, etc.—Fiction. 3. Conduct of life—Fiction.]
I. Os, Erik van. II. Gerritsen, Paula, ill. III. Title.

PZ7.L619No 2004
[E]-dc22   2004046932

by Elle van Lieshout & Erik van Os

ILLUSTRATED BY

Paula Gerritsen

The Nothing King

FRONT STREET ✌ LEMNISCAAT

Just before dark King Bear found the place he was looking for: an apartment for rent, on the outskirts of town, on the third floor of an old building.

King Bear parked his carriage and fed his horses. Then he unloaded his stuff and moved everything inside.

"Why, Your Majesty," said the owner, "where are your servants?"

"Not here," the king said happily, "but maybe you can help me with the carpet?"

That night, King Bear had no servant to brush his teeth, no lady-in-waiting to scrub his back, no valet to comb his hair...

He took a bath all by himself, he put on his pajamas all by himself, and he went to bed all by himself.

It was great!

The next day King Bear bought —all by himself—a carton of milk, a cheese sandwich, an apple, a carrot for his rabbit, and a watering can for his pansy in the shop at the corner.

He whistled the whole way back to his new apartment.

King Bear and his rabbit enjoyed a royal meal on the balcony.

He listened to the noises of the city in the distance: a chugging train, the soft drone of cars, playing children...

King Bear closed his eyes and let the warm wind ruffle his hair.

Life is beautiful up here, he thought.

In the afternoon King Bear said, "Come on, rabbit, the weather is perfect for a walk."
He leashed his rabbit and went to the park.

Along the path an old lady stopped him. "Your Majesty," she said, "why are you strolling through a public park with your rabbit on a leash? Shouldn't you be at the palace?"

King Bear looked at his rabbit.

"What was I thinking?" he answered her.

He unleashed the rabbit and they happily continued on their way.

When King Bear came back to his apartment the mayor was standing beside his carriage.

"Your Majesty," the mayor said, "why is your royal carriage parked on this common street?"

King Bear considered his carriage. "You're right," he said, "it's only taking up space." He took the horses to a meadow and put the carriage up for sale.

The next day his prime minister came by.

"Hey," King Bear said, pleasantly surprised, "I didn't expect to see you here."

The prime minister coughed and said, "We can't do without you, Your Majesty. There is a lot of reigning to be done!"

King Bear nodded.

"You are right," he said, and then he threw his royal robe around the prime minister. "You take care of it."

At first the prime minister looked a bit confused. Then he gathered the robe around him and started back to the palace.

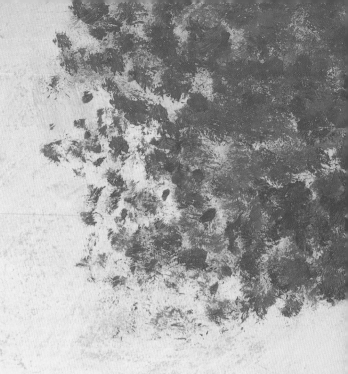

A little later the queen was at his door.

"Bear, you're acting strangely!" she told him. "How very rude of you to leave me alone in that big palace."

"You're right, my dear," King Bear said. "Move in with me, here—in my pleasant apartment."

"Here?" the queen said. She blinked her eyes. "In this little place?"

King Bear nodded.

"Impossible," the queen said. She shook her head, blew him a kiss, and went back to the palace.

A pity, King Bear thought. But it's a free country.

He brought his rabbit out on the balcony and turned his pansy to the sun.

Laughter rang out from down in the street. King Bear looked over the railing of his balcony.

Neighbors looked up at him and laughed. "Ha ha, he calls himself a king! But he has absolutely nothing; no queen, no palace, no servants, not even a royal carriage. He is a nothing king."

"A nothing king!"

"A nothing king!"

Their taunting echoed off the walls.

King Bear thought about what they were saying. Was he a nothing king?

He looked up and felt the sun on his face. He petted his rabbit and studied his pansy.

He began to laugh. "I have a rabbit, a pansy, and a balcony in the sun. How can you call that nothing?"

He laughed and laughed and laughed. He let the soft spring air fill his lungs. He gave his rabbit a carrot, watered his pansy, and ate his sandwich on his balcony in the sun.

The neighbors grew quiet and went back to their homes.

And just before dark the queen arrived at his doorstep. Nothing could be better!

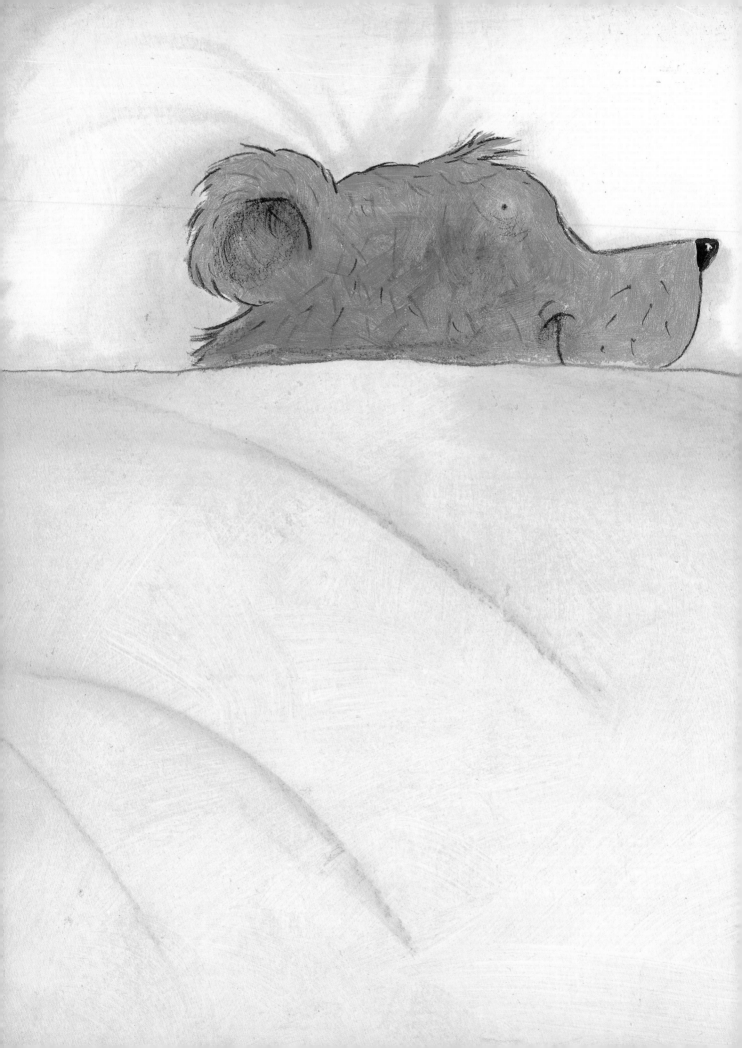